D1572823

·DIRTY·DAVE·

by Nette Hilton · illustrated by Roland Harvey

ORCHARD BOOKS · NEW YORK

Text copyright © 1987 by Nette Hilton. Illustrations copyright © 1987 by Roland Harvey. First American Edition 1990 published by Orchard Books.

First published in Australia by The Five Mile Press

Orchard Books, A division of Franklin Watts, Inc., 387 Park Avenue South, New York, NY 10016.

Manufactured in the United States of America. Printed by Gereral Offset Co., Inc. Bound by Horowitz / Rae. The text of this book is set in Nicholas Cochin. The illustrations are pen and ink and watercolor which were camera separated and reproduced in four colors. Book design by Mina Greenstein

2   4   6   8   10   9   7   5   3   1

Library of Congress Cataloging-in-Publication Data. Hilton, Nette. [Dirty Dave the Bushranger]. Dirty Dave / by Nette Hilton; illustrated by Roland Harvey. — 1st American Ed.   p.   cm.   Original title: Dirty Dave the Bushranger. Summary: Members of an outlaw family gain acceptance from the public because of the fine clothes their father makes for them. ISBN 0-531-05861-1. ISBN 0-531-08461-2 (lib. bdg.)   [1. Robbers and outlaws — Fiction. 2. Clothing and dress — Fiction.]   I. Harvey, Roland, ill.   II. Title.   PZ7.H56775Di   1990   [E] — dc20   89-35402   CIP   AC

·DIRTY·DAVE·

Dave was an outlaw.
He was tough.

Sue was his sister.
She was rough.

Maude was his mother.
She was fierce.

Dan was his dad.
He liked to sew.

Dave roared, "Stop!"
Sue bellowed, "Whoa!"
Maude hollered, "Hands up!"

But Dan stayed at home.

Dave shouted, "Money!"

Sue demanded, "Jewels!"

Maude wanted, "Candy, please!"

And Dan sewed and sewed.

"Go!" shouted Dave.
"Git!" shouted Sue.
"Hurry up!" said Maude.
  But the travelers wouldn't go.
"Stay," said one,
  "there's something we must know."

"Stay?" asked Dave.
"What?" asked Sue.
"Why?" asked Maude.

"Who is your tailor?
That shirt's really fine!"

"Look at his trousers!"

"I wish her dress were mine!"

"Who does your stitching?
We'd pay a lot to know."

Dave looked tough.
Sue looked confused.

Maude rolled her eyes.
"Their dad loves to sew."

Now...
Dave models clothes.
He's still tough.
Sue's a model too.
But not quite as rough.

Maude's still their mom.
She still loves sweets.

And Dan stays at home,

and sews and sews and sews.